Ned the Gnat

To Marsha, Mike, Marko, and Max
I hope you enjoy reading my book!
  Love,
    David

Copyright © 2018 David Baer
All rights reserved
First Edition

PAGE PUBLISHING, INC.
New York, NY

First originally published by Page Publishing, Inc. 2018

ISBN 978-1-64214-715-5 (Paperback)
ISBN 978-1-64424-056-4 (Hardcover)
ISBN 978-1-64214-716-2 (Digital)

Printed in the United States of America

Ned the Gnat

DAVID BAER

Hi, I'm Ned the gnat.

I have a best friend named Fred.

Fred and I love to buzz in your ear, nose,
and mouth, then we like to go south.
We love to sting, nag, and bite.
And believe me, we put up a fight!
Every time someone swats at me,
I just laugh and say I'm no flea.

But believe me, I can bother you,
Especially when I get in your shoe.

Every time you walk, I bite at your feet,

And wait till I get in your bed sheets.

You will toss, turn, and cry.

But I am no fly.

Flies buzz around,

But I will stay and make you frown.

It pleases me the more I get under your skin.

Then I will move up to your shin.

It makes me so happy to buzz in your ear

Because I have no fear!

But when I get people mad,

I don't get sad.

People say I just want to get rid of this gnat,

but it isn't as easy as that!

I love to frustrate people.

It is just what I do.

It is nothing new.

But Fred and I get along great.

We even like to hang out late!

We like to nag, nag, and nag.

We can be quite a drag.

If I ever have kids,

They will do the same

Because us gnats have no shame!

My mom and dad taught me

everything I know.

But believe me, it's no show!

I don't play,
And I won't go away!
Us gnats don't hug and kiss.
We give people no bliss.

I like to come out when the weather is hot.

Go away, I will not.

So now we must say goodbye.

And leave on a high!

But Fred and I will be back for another attack!

Don't get me wrong, us gnats are strong.

So goodbye again.

Fred and I had fun!

So, kids, please give your parents
a big hug and kiss.
And maybe Ned the gnat and
Fred will give you a miss!

THE END

About the Author

Growing up, David Baer's mother read him Dr. Seuss books, and he was fascinated with his writing style. That's why David decided to write a rhyming children's story about a gnat. His English teacher in Cocoa Beach High thought that he had a lot of talent for writing. So he has written this book for children and adults to enjoy!

CPSIA information can be obtained
at www.ICGtesting.com
Printed in the USA
BVHW02s0044200918
528001BV00011B/81/P